The Little Mermaid

Hans Christian Andersen

Illustrated by Hubert Sergeant
Translated from the original Danish text
by Marlee Alex

WORD INC.

Within the fairy-tale treasury which has come into the world's possession, there is no doubt Hans Christian Andersen's stories are of outstanding character. Their symbolism is rich with character values. From his early childhood in the town of Odense, Denmark, until his death in Copenhagen, Hans Christian Andersen (1805-1875) wrote approximately 150 stories and tales. The thread in Andersen's stories is one of optimism which has given hope and inspiration to people all over the world. It is in this spirit that the Tales of Hans Christian Andersen are published.

Far out at sea, the water is as blue as the bluest cornflower, and as clear as glass. It is very deep, so deep that no anchor can possibly reach the bottom. It would require a great many church towers, stacked on top of each other, to reach from the floor of the sea to its surface.

Now, you should not imagine the floor of the sea as a naked, white sandy bottom. No, indeed! An amazing variety of trees and plants grow there. Their branches are so resilient they move like living creatures at the least movement in the water. The fish, both small and great, dart between them just like birds in the air. And this is where the sea-folk lived.

At the very deepest place lay the sea-king's palace. Its walls were made of coral; its long, pointed windows of transparent amber. The roof was composed of oyster shells which opened and closed with the currents of the water, and in each shell lay a shining pearl. The least of these pearls would have been considered a great treasure in the crown of a queen.

The sea-king had been a widower for many years. His aging mother kept house for him. She was a wise woman, but very proud of her lineage. She wore twelve oysters on her tail, whereas others of royal blood were only allowed six. Otherwise, she deserved much praise, especially because she

loved her granddaughters, the small sea-princesses, so dearly.

There were six sea-princesses, and each was lovelier than the one before. The youngest was, of course, the most beautiful of all. Her skin was as soft as a rose petal, her eyes as green as the deepest sea. But just like all the others, she had no feet. Her body ended in a fishtail.

All day long the princesses played in the palace, where living flowers grew out of the walls. The big, amber windows were opened so fish could swim in and out. They swam right up to the small princesses, ate out of their hands and allowed themselves to be petted.

Beyond the palace walls was a large garden with dark red and blue trees. The fruit glittered like gold and the flowers flickered like fire because the petals and leaves were in constant motion. The sand in the garden was very fine, but it was deep blue like live coal dust. A strange azure haze lay over everything. When the water was calm you could see the glimmer of the sun above. It was like a crimson cup from which a stream of light was poured out.

Each of the princesses had a little plot in the garden which she could cultivate exactly as she pleased. One of them made her flower bed in the shape of a whale; another preferred hers to look

5

like a mermaid. But the youngest made hers perfectly round like the sun and planted only red flowers. She was a mysterious child, quiet and thoughtful. Her sisters decorated their flower beds with things they had found on sunken ships, but she kept only a marble pillar in hers. It was the statue of a boy. She planted a rose-colored weeping willow beside it. The willow grew lush and wild. The shadow which it cast upon the floor of the sea was violet-colored, and was in constant motion just like its branches. It looked like the roots and the leaves of the willow were kissing each other.

The princesses' grandmother, the aging sea-queen, was fond of telling stories; and none were more popular among the mermaids than those about the human world above. The youngest mermaid, especially, enjoyed hearing how the flowers above had a fragrance, which they did not have on the floor of the ocean. And in the forests, the "fish" which flitted among the branches could sing ever so sweetly. (Grandmother always called the little birds "fish," for otherwise the mermaids would not understand, since they had never seen a bird.) "On your fifteenth birhtday," promised the old queen, "you will be allowed to swim to the surface of the sea. You can sit in the moonlight on the rocks and watch the big ships sail by. You may even get a glimpse of forests and towns."

None of the sisters sighed with as much longing as the youngest, she who had the longest time to wait. Many an evening this dreamy little mermaid stood by an open window and looked up through the deep blue water. She could see the pale shimmer of the moon and stars. Sometimes a black cloud sailed past, but she knew it was either a whale swimming above or a ship filled with people, people who would never have imagined that a sweet mermaid stood below, stretching her white hands out towards the keel of their ship.

At last the eldest princess turned fifteen and made her trip to the surface of the ocean. When she returned she had hundreds of things to tell. The nicest of all, she said, was lying on a sandbar in the moonlight and watching the city beyond. Lights twinkled like hundreds of stars. The hum of city life was like music. She could see church towers, and hear the bells chiming.

The following year, the second sister swam up through the water. Her head rose above the surface just as the sun was setting. The sky was golden; the clouds were pink and violet. A trail of wild swans flew over the water past the sinking sun. The princess swam after them, and watched the rosy glow of the heavens drown in the sea.

The third sister was the boldest of them all. She swam up a wide river that emptied into the sea. Green banks covered by grapevines bordered the river. Castles and farms peeked out through the forests. Then, in a little inlet, she saw naked children splashing in the water. Oh, how she wanted to play with them! But as she swam closer, they were frightened away. She would never forget those sweet children who were able to swim even though they had no fishtail.

The fourth sister stayed out in the middle of the wild ocean on her fifteenth birthday, but insisted it was the nicest place of all. She could see for miles around. The sky above her was like a crystal globe. The fun-loving dolphins turned somersaults, and the great whales sprayed water high into the air like hundreds of splashing fountains.

When the fifth sister's turn came it was winter, so she saw what none of the others had seen! The sea was green. Large icebergs floated around her, as white as pearls. They sparkled like diamonds. Then they seemed to take on strange, animal-like shapes in the moonlight. She climbed up on the largest of them and watched in delight as a furious storm crossed the ocean.

The sisters were impressed by all the new and beautiful things they saw the first time they swam to the surface. After a while, however, when they could swim anywhere, anytime they wanted, these things no longer fascinated them. They admitted there was no place as wonderful as home.

Still, there were many evenings when the five sisters took each other by the hand and rose in a long line through the water. Whenever a storm was brewing and they saw a ship in danger, they would swim in front of it and sing about how beautiful it was at the bottom of the sea. On these occasions, the youngest sister was left alone at home feeling sad and sorry. But mermaids have no tears; they cannot cry. So the little mermaid suffered much more painfully than we can imagine.

At last, she too, turned fifteen! Her grandmother said, "Come, let me dress you up as I did each of your sisters." A garland of white lilies was set on her head; and each petal of each flower was half a pearl!

"Goodbye!" waved the little mermaid happily as she rose like a bubble through the water. Reaching the surface, she saw the ocean was completely quiet. The evening stars twinkled in the sky. Then she spied a large three-masted ship with her sails unfurled. The sound of music and song came from the ship. Hundreds of swaying, colored lamps lined its deck, like flags of all nations, waving in the breeze.

The little mermaid rode the waves beside the ship, watching the festivities onboard as the evening grew late. The colored lamps were finally put out, and the fireworks finished. It grew quiet upon the ship, but from deep below the sea there was a rumbling sound. The waves grew in size and strength. Dark clouds appeared out of nowhere. Lightning cracked in the distance. The ship began to rock wildly in the heaving sea. It creaked and groaned until, at last, the mast snapped in two like a reed. The ship was slung onto its side and water filled the cabin.

One moment it was so dark the little mermaid could see nothing at all. The next moment she could see by a lightning flash all the people tumbling out of the sinking ship. Just as the ship disappeared into the sea she caught sight of the young prince. The planks and splintered boards being tossed on the waves could have crushed her, but she swam between them, dived into the water, then reappeared between the waves. She reached the prince just as he was giving up the fight against the stormy sea. She lifted his head above the water and let the waves drive the two of them away.

By morning, the storm had passed. There was not a splinter of the ship to be seen. As the sun rose, the pale cheeks of the young man began to blush. The little mermaid kissed him on his forehead and stroked his hair. She thought he looked like the boy carved upon the marble pillar in her little garden. She kissed him again, desperately hoping he would live.

On the horizon, a lovely coast line appeared. The little mermaid swam to the shore and laid the prince carefully on the sand with his head in the warm sunshine. Suddenly, bells started ringing from a nearby building. Girls ran into the garden close to the beach. The little mermaid dived back into the sea to hide. She stayed behind a rock which jutted out of the water, and camouflaged herself with sea foam. Then she watched to see what would happen to the poor young prince.

One of the girls wandered towards the beach. When she saw the boy lying soaking wet in the sand she was frightened. The prince opened his eyes and smiled at her. But he had no smile for the little mermaid, for he did not know that she was the one who had rescued him. They led him away, and the sad little mermaid swam sorrowfully back to her father's palace.

At home she had always been quiet and sensitive, but now she became even more so. When her sisters asked what she had experienced on her trip above, she said nothing. Sometimes she would swim through the sea to the place where she had left the prince. She saw how the fruit along the coast ripened and was picked. She saw how the snow on the mountaintops melted, but she never saw the prince. Each time, she returned home even sadder than the time before.

At last the little mermaid could no longer bear it. She told one of her sisters, and then almost immediately, the others knew as well. No more than these five were told, besides a couple of other mermaids who promised not to tell anyone except their closest friends. It turned out that one of these friends knew who the prince was and where his kingdom could be found.

"Come little sister!" said the other princesses. With their arms around each other's shoulders, they rose in a line up out of the sea just in front of the prince's castle. The castle was built of pale, polished stone. Its marble staircase went right down to the sea.

Now that the little mermaid knew where the prince lived, she returned to his castle many times. She swam much nearer to the shore than her sisters dared. On many an evening she watched as he stood alone on his balcony. Other times she watched him sail in his magnificent ship.

Sometimes she heard the fishermen talk about how good the young prince was. It made her happy that she had saved his life. She remembered how securely his head had rested against her shoulder. Yet he knew nothing about her; he could not even dream about her.

The little mermaid grew to love humans more and more. She wished she could live among them. Their world was much larger than hers. Their countries stretched over forest and field farther than she could see. There was so much she wished to know. Her sisters could not answer all her questions, so she asked her grandmother, "If humans do not drown, do they go on living? Do they ever die as we do here in the sea?"

"Yes, they must also die," answered her grandmother, "and their lifetime is shorter than ours. We live to be three hundred years old, but when we die we have no graves among our loved ones. We become foam on the ocean. We have no eternal soul which can go on living. But humans have a soul which lives forever. It rises through the air to the shining stars, to unknown, wonderful places which we will never see."

"Why weren't we given an eternal soul? I would give all of my three hundred years for just one day among humans and a chance to share in the heavenly world! Can't I do anything to win an eternal soul, Grandmother?"

"There is only one way," answered the old woman gently. "If a man, somewhere, sometime, fell so much in love with you that you came to mean more to him than his father or mother, if he vowed to be faithful to you forever; then, at the moment the two of you were married, his soul would flood into your body and you would be filled with human happiness. He can give you a soul and yet keep his own. But it will never happen! No human wants a wife with a fishtail! On earth one must have two clumsy pillars called legs in order to be thought beautiful!"

The little mermaid sighed and looked sadly at her fishtail.

"Let us be happy," said the old woman. "We can splash and swirl for three hundred years. It is time

14

enough. And tonight is the palace ball!"

That evening a broad, swift current flowed through the ballroom at the palace. Upon this current the mermen and mermaids danced to the music of their own singing. Humans do not possess such beautiful voices. The little mermaid sang most beautifully of them all. They applauded her, and for a moment she felt happy, for she knew she had the loveliest voice on earth or in the sea. Her happiness, however, was brief. For she could not get the prince out of her mind, nor could she quell the longing for an eternal soul.

While the others danced, the little mermaid silently left her father's palace and headed for the house of the sea-witch. Though it was a fearful thing to do, she was willing to risk anything to win the desire of her heart. She swam towards the turbulent whirlpool behind which the witch lived. There were no flowers or sea grass along the way. As she approached the whirlpool she saw it was like a mill wheel which tore at everything, carrying it down into the depths below. Beyond this was a steamy, bubbling bog, and a strange forest of animal-like trees. The branches of these trees were long and subtle like snake heads, each of them covered with slimy fingers extending like wriggling worms. Every bit of the trees moved constantly.

Everything they could grasp onto, they twisted and never let go of.

The little mermaid shrunk back in fright. Her heart beat wildly. On the verge of turning back, she remembered the prince and the human soul she wished so desperately to win, and her courage returned. She believed the sea-witch could help her.

She wound her hair close to her head so the trees could not grab it, folded both arms tightly across her chest and flew through the forest as fast as a fish can fly through the water. The horrid trees stretched their wriggling arms and fingers toward her. In her flight she noticed each of them held something they had long since captured. Skeletons of people who had drowned peeked out of their arms. Ship oars, treasure chests, animals, and even a little strangled mermaid lay tangled in their grasp.

At last she arrived at the clearing where the sea-witch's house lay. It was built of the white bones of drowned sailors. Outside, fat eels tumbled in play.

"I know very well what you want!" smirked the sea-witch. "And it is stupid of you! But I will help you anyway, my dear princess, because it will bring you grief and unhappiness. You wish to get rid of your fishtail and have two stumps to walk on instead! You hope the prince will fall in love with you so you can win an eternal soul. You have come at the right time. At sunrise tomorrow I would not be able to help you for another year."

"Here is what I will do," she continued. "I will make you a magic potion. You must swim with it to the shore and drink it before sunrise. Then your fishtail will divide in two and become legs. Be assured, it will be painful! It will feel as if a sword were passing through your body. The graceful sway of a mermaid will remain with you when you walk and dance, but each step you take will feel like sharp knives piercing your feet. Are you willing to suffer all this?"

"Yes," answered the little mermaid with a wavering voice.

"But remember!" added the witch. "When you have once taken the shape of a human, you can never be a mermaid again. You can never return to your sisters nor to your father's palace. And if you fail to win the love of the prince you will get no eternal soul! The first morning after he is wed to another, your heart will break and you will become foam on the waves of the sea."

"Let it be," whispered the little mermaid. She was as pale as death.

"You must pay me, of course; and I want no small reward! You probably think you will enchant the prince with your beautiful voice, the most valuable thing you possess. However, my potion is costly. I will have the best you own in payment!"

"But if you take my voice, what will I have left?" asked the little mermaid.

"You will have your lovely figure, your graceful walk, and your whispering eyes. With those you can surely capture the heart of a man. Have you lost courage?"

"No. I will go through with it," said the little mermaid as she trembled.

The witch set her big, black kettle over the fire. She scoured it first with eels, then scratched herself in the chest and let her black blood drip into it. She continued adding new ingredients as she stirred. When the potion came to a boil, it sounded like the crying of crocodiles. When it was finished, it was transparent as water.

"Here it is!" cried the witch as she cut off the tongue of the little mermaid. Now the poor sea-princess could neither speak nor sing.

She would have to fly again through the strange undersea forest. But this time the trees shrunk back when they saw the shining drink she carried. It twinkled like a star. She continued through the sea, past her father's palace. It was dark and quiet. The little mermaid would have to leave her family forever, now. Her heart felt as if it would break. Silently, she took one flower from each of the flowerbeds of her sisters, threw a thousand kisses towards the palace and rose through the deep blue sea.

19

The sun had not yet risen when she reached the marble stairs leading to the prince's castle. Drinking the burning potion in the moonlight, she fainted from pain and lay as though dead. At sunrise she woke up under the steady gaze of the prince. Bashfully, she avoided his black eyes, and looked down. Her fishtail was gone. In its place were two pretty legs, half hidden by her long hair.

The prince asked her who she was. She could only look sadly but gently at him with her dark green eyes. He took her by the hand and led her up into his castle. Each step was just as painful as the witch had predicted, but she suffered it gladly. She rose up the stairs as light as a bubble, and everyone who saw her admired the graceful way she carried herself.

The little mermaid was clothed in the finest silk and linen. Then slave girls came out and sang for the royal family. The prince clapped for them enthusiastically, but the little mermaid grew sad. She knew she had once sung more beautifully than they. She thought, "If only he

knew that in order to be with him I have sacrificed
my voice for all eternity."

As the slave girls started dancing, the little
mermaid lifted her pretty arms, rose to her toes, and
swayed across the floor, dancing as none before had
ever danced. Her loveliness became more obvious
with each movement, and her eyes spoke more
deeply to the heart of the prince than had the
song of the slave girls.

At night the little mermaid was given permission to sleep outside the door of the prince on a velvet pillow. By day she rode horses with him through the forests, and climbed mountains with him to watch the clouds float by below. In the evenings she went out on the marble steps to cool her burning feet in the cold sea water. At these times she thought about her loved ones below.

One night her sisters came, arm in arm, through the water. They were singing ever so sorrowfully. The little mermaid waved to them. They told her how unhappy she had made them. Each night thereafter they visited her. One night she saw her grandmother and her father, the sea-king, wearing his crown. They stretched out their hands towards her from afar, for they dared not to come too close to land.

Day by day, the little mermaid became more dear to the prince. He loved her as one loves a little sister, but it did not occur to him to make her his queen. "You are the most loving person I've ever known," he said. "And you resemble a young girl I saw once when I was driven ashore after a shipwreck. That girl saved my life and she is the only one I could possibly love in all this world. You bring the memory of her face back to my heart."

"He does not know that it was I who saved his life!" thought the little mermaid. "It was I who carried him through the sea and watched over him. I even saw the girl who found him, the girl he loves more than me." The little mermaid sighed deeply, for she could not cry. At least, I am the one who is with him now. I will care for him, love him, devote my life to him."

One day the king and queen announced the prince was to be married. He was to have the daughter of the neighboring king for a wife. A great ship was equipped for his trip. "My parents want me to see the princess," he said to the little mermaid. "But they cannot force me to make her my bride. I could never love anyone except the girl who saved my life. And I will never see her again, I'm sure. If I am to marry, I would sooner marry you, my child." Then he played with her long hair, and laid his head on her heart. Her heart began to dream in earnest about human happiness and an eternal soul.

As they sailed toward the neighboring kingdom, the prince told the little mermaid about the storms at sea, the moods of the ocean, and the extraordinary fish at the bottom of it, the ones his divers had seen. She smiled as he spoke, for no one knew better than she did what lay on the bottom of the sea.

In the clear night, when all the others were asleep, the little mermaid sat at the bow of the ship and looked down through the clear water. She almost thought she saw her father's palace. Then her sisters appeared, looking terribly sad, and wringing their hands. She waved to them, smiled and tried to let them know that she was well and happy.

The following morning, the ship sailed into harbor. All the churchbells were ringing to welcome the prince. When the princess came into sight, the little mermaid admitted she had never seen a lovelier young woman. Her skin was smooth and delicate, her eyes were cheerful and loyal.

"It is you!" declared the prince to the young woman. "You're the one who saved me when I was washed ashore!" The prince embraced his blushing bride. He turned to the little mermaid and said, "My wildest dreams have come true! Surely, you will rejoice with me, for no one loves me as you do." The little mermaid kissed his hand, but felt as if her heart would break. His wedding day would mean her death.

Heralds rode through the city streets proclaiming the engagement. The bride and groom took each other's hand and received the blessing of the bishop.

The little mermaid carried the veil of the bride, but her ears did not hear the festive music, nor did her eyes witness the sacred moment of marriage. She was absorbed in thoughts about all she had lost in the world.

That evening the bride and bridegroom boarded the ship among banners and fireworks. The colored lamps were lit and the sailors danced upon the deck. The little mermaid was reminded of the first time she had seen the prince. She began to whirl and sway to the music. Never had she danced so wonderfully. She didn't even feel the piercing knives tearing at her feet, for her heart was in much greater pain. She knew it was the last evening she would see the one for whom she had left family and home, for whom she had given away her voice and suffered daily agony. And he would never know.

The festivity on the ship lasted until well past midnight. The little mermaid laughed and danced, though feelings of death filled her heart. Finally the bride and bridegroom retired for the night in the beautiful tent. All became quiet. The little mermaid leaned against the railing and looked eastward towards dawn. She knew the first sun rays would kill her.

Then she saw her sisters rise out of the sea. They were as pale as she. Their hair no longer waved in the wind, for it had been cut off. "We have given our hair to the sea-witch so you would not have to

die tonight. She has given us a knife. Before sunrise you must drive it into the heart of the prince, and when his blood sprinkles onto your feet you will become a mermaid again and live out your three hundred years. Hurry! He or you must die! Grandmother has mourned for you; all her white hair has fallen out from grief. Kill the prince and return! Hurry! Don't you see that red stripe across the sky?" The princesses threw the knife on board the ship, gave a strange, deep sigh, then disappeared among the waves.

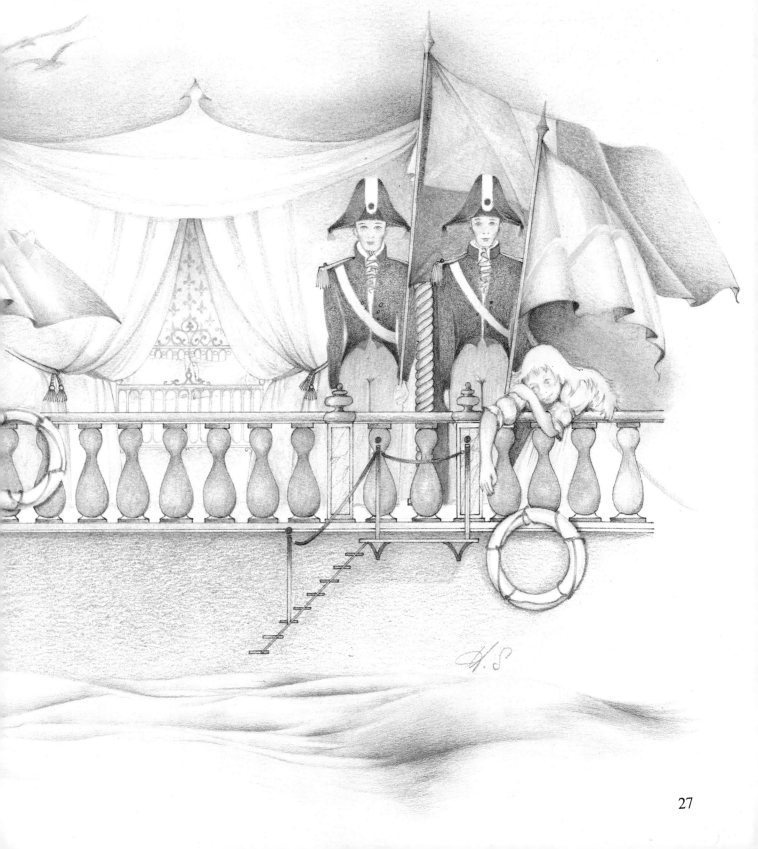

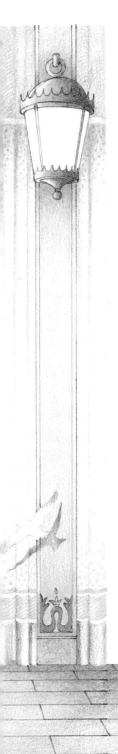
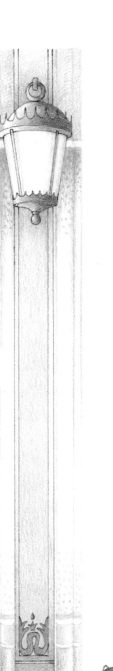

The little mermaid drew aside the heavy curtain from the door of the tent and saw the lovely bride asleep with her head resting upon the prince's chest.

She bent and kissed the prince, glanced back at the sky as it grew lighter, and tightened her grip on the knife. She looked again at the prince. In his sleep he murmured the name of his bride; she was the only one in his dreams.

The knife quivered in the hand of the little mermaid. Suddenly, she turned and cast it far out into the sea. The waves turned red where it fell, like splattered drops of blood upon the water. Once more the little mermaid gave a half-glazed glance at the prince. Then she ran across the deck and threw herself into the sea.

The sun rose. Its rays fell warm and kindly on the deathly cold ocean foam. But the little mermaid did not feel death. She saw the sun above, and then, hundreds of gracefully swaying spirits floating over her. She could see through them; beyond, to the white sail of the ship, and the red clouds in the sky. Their voices were melodious, and so spiritual no human ear could hear them, just as no human eye could see these spirits. They had no wings, yet swayed blithely in the air. The little mermaid felt herself rise out of the foam with a body like theirs.

"Where am I going?" she asked. Her voice chimed musically like the others. No music on earth or under the sea would ever be able to duplicate it.

"With the daughters of the air!" answered the others. "You, little mermaid, were given no eternal soul, but like us, you are able to create one because you have a loving, giving heart. We fly to hot and humid parts of the world and fan a cool breeze upon the inhabitants plagued by disease. We spread the fragrance of flowers through the air and bring healing. When we have done as much good as we possibly can for three hundred years we will win an eternal soul, and take part in the eternal bliss which was meant for humans. You have tried with all your heart to do the same. You have suffered much and endured to the end. Rise to the world of the spirits of the air!"

The little mermaid lifted her arms toward the sun of God. Then she felt for the first time in her life, a refreshing flow of tears on her cheeks. As she rose over the ship, she saw the prince and his beautiful bride staring regretfully into the sea, as if they knew she had cast herself into the waves. Although unseen, she kissed the prince and smiled warmly at him. Then, together with the other children of the air, she stepped upon a passing pink cloud and continued her journey.

THE LITTLE MERMAID   STUDY KEY

Explaining the story:

The Little Mermaid is the story of someone who felt there must be more to life than pretty things and having fun. She was willing to risk losing everything for the love of a prince and for the hope of winning eternal life. Her story shows that nothing in the world is stronger than love, not even suffering or death. At the end of the story she gave her life for the prince with no hope of receiving anything in return. She did not expect that by this final act of love she would gain what she dreamed of most ... eternal life.

Talking about the truth of the story:

1. How was the little mermaid different than her sisters?
2. How did she risk her life the first time to save the prince?
3. Did the little mermaid dream most about her lovely undersea world, falling in love with a prince, or winning eternal life?
4. What kinds of suffering did the little mermaid endure in order to make her dream come true?

Applying the truth of the story:

1. You must have many dreams and wishes. What is your biggest dream?
2. Most people try to avoid suffering as much as possible. What are some of the good things that happen when you accept suffering which cannot be changed? What happens if you don't learn to accept it? In what ways does suffering make you stronger? Are you better able to help others who are suffering once you have suffered?
3. This story contains a secret lesson about what happens when you give all of yourself for the sake of another. What is that lesson?